Grumpy Pumpkins

YOUNG YEARLING BOOKS YOU WILL ENJOY:

The Pee Wee Scout books by Judy Delton

COOKIES AND CRUTCHES

CAMP GHOST-AWAY

LUCKY DOG DAYS

BLUE SKIES, FRENCH FRIES

GRUMPY PUMPKINS

PEANUT-BUTTER PILGRIMS

A PEE WEE CHRISTMAS

Grumpy Pumpkins

JUDY DELTON

Illustrated by Alan Tiegreen

A YOUNG YEARLING BOOK

Published by
Dell Publishing
a division of
Bantam Doubleday Dell Publishing Group, Inc.
666 Fifth Avenue
New York, New York 10103

ISBN: 0-440-40065-1

Printed in the United States of America

October 1988

10 9

FOR JINA, WHO ALONG LIFE'S ROUTE
WAS, LONG AGO, MY BROWNIE SCOUT

Contents

CHAPTER 1

Halloween Plans

"Hurry, hurry," called Mrs. Peters, the Pee Wee Scout leader. "Run between the raindrops."

The Pee Wee Scouts hurried off the bus and raced one another to Mrs. Peters's open door.

Roger White got there first. He was the biggest.

"That's not fair!" shouted Sonny Betz. "You've got the longest legs."

Molly Duff and Lisa Ronning ran past Sonny and got to the door next.

1

"How can we run between the drops?" said Lisa, giggling. "There isn't room."

"That's a figure of speech." Mrs. Peters laughed. "Like 'Make hay while the sun shines.' "

"We can't make hay today," said Sonny. "How do you make hay anyway?"

All the Pee Wees laughed.

Pretty soon all the Scouts were there. It felt good to be in Mrs. Peters's house. Warm and dry.

There was a fire in the fireplace. And cups of cocoa sat on the table.

Lucky, their mascot, was there. And Tiny, Mrs. Peters's dog.

The dogs liked Scout meetings. Sometimes they got part of a cookie. Or a bite of cheese and cracker.

And some Scout would always rub their ears and want to play fetch.

The Pee Wees were in second grade.

Most of them were seven.

They did lots of good deeds.

And they had fun.

They even earned badges to wear on their shirts. They all had bright red Pee Wee scarves to wear around their necks.

The Scouts gathered around the table and drank cocoa. It warmed them up. They forgot how rainy and dark it was outside.

"I'll bet everyone knows what month this is," said Mrs. Peters.

There was a paper tablecloth on the table with pictures of pumpkins on it. The napkins had little pumpkins in the corners too.

"Halloween!" said Tracy Barnes. "It's Halloween month."

"Halloween isn't a month," scoffed Rachel, combing her hair and snapping her barrette.

"It's the month of October," said Patty Baker shyly.

"Yeah, Patty Cake!" shouted Roger. "The baker's man knows what month it is!"

"Good, Patty," said Mrs. Peters. "October is a damp, dark month. An autumn month. A month with Halloween in it."

"Oooooo!" wailed Kenny Baker like a moaning ghost. Kenny was Patty's twin brother.

The Pee Wee Scouts chased one another around the room, making sounds like ghosts and goblins.

"Can we have a Halloween party?" asked Molly. "A Pee Wee costume party?"

Mrs. Peters smiled. "That is one of the things I wanted to talk about," she said. "I have a couple of Halloween ideas. The first one is that this year I thought we'd go to Mr. Riley's pumpkin farm. We will each pick our own pumpkin."

The Scouts looked surprised.

"That way," said Mrs. Peters, "we will each have a nice fresh pumpkin. And you can choose it yourself, and pick it right off the vine."

When Mrs. Peters said "vine" Sonny looked puzzled. "How do they get on

vines?" he asked. "I thought pumpkins came in cans. From the store."

Now the Pee Wees really laughed.

He probably doesn't even know where babies come from, thought Molly. He probably thinks the stork is bringing Mrs. Peters's baby! Molly smiled.

"Farmers grow pumpkins in fields, Sonny," said Mrs. Peters kindly. "From seeds. Pumpkin seeds."

Sonny looked as if he did not believe her.

"And now for the other news," said Mrs. Peters.

CHAPTER 2

A Visit to Crestwood

The Pee Wees sat up straight. This must be the big news. The news about the party!

"You were right," said Mrs. Peters. "I think we should have a costume party for Halloween."

The Scouts cheered.

"Arf! Arf!" barked Tiny. Lucky barked too. "Yip! Yip!"

"I want to be a ballerina," said Rachel. "My mom knows this great place where they make costumes to order."

"I'm coming as the President of the

8

United States!" shouted Kevin. "Or maybe a TV rock star."

Kevin has big ideas, thought Molly.

"I might come as a Pee Wee Scout," said Tim Noon.

"Dumb," said Sonny. "We're Pee Wee Scouts already."

But Molly knew why Tim wanted to come as a Scout. His family was on welfare. He probably couldn't afford a costume.

Molly felt sorry for Tim. Maybe she could make him a costume. It would be awful to come as a Scout when he already was one.

The Pee Wees shouted out more ideas about what they would wear. And who they would be.

Mrs. Peters held up her hand. "At a costume party no one should know who you are," she reminded them. "We want

9

it to be a surprise. We must all wear a mask with our costume."

"I'm not really coming as a ballerina," said Rachel quickly. "I just made that up."

"Me too," said Kevin. "I have a new idea. A secret idea."

The Scouts were so excited, they couldn't sit still. Molly shivered with excitement.

"I haven't finished my news!" called Mrs. Peters over the noise. "The rest of the news is that the party won't be here at my house."

"Will it be at school?" asked Kevin. "Yuck, I don't want to go to a party at school."

"It's too cold for the park," said Roger. "It has to be inside."

"It will be inside," said Mrs. Peters. "But it will be inside a nursing home. My idea was to have a good time ourselves, and also give the people there a good time. We will make their Halloween fun too. Won't that be a good deed for Troop 23 to do?"

The Pee Wees stopped smiling. Molly pictured the old people in beds. The grandpas with long beards. The grandmas with no teeth. The nurses with their pills and needles.

"It doesn't sound like a party to me," whispered Rachel. "Sick people. Old and wrinkled."

"Most of the people are not sick," said Mrs. Peters. "They are lonely and some have no visitors. We will cheer them up. We'll play games with them. Eat with them. They will be in costume too."

Then Mrs. Peters added, "There will be a prize for the best costume. One for the best Pee Wee costume, and one for the best grown-up costume. Try to make

11

the costume yourself if you can. Just buy the mask."

Molly pictured a goblin with a long gray beard.

Roger wondered how a man in a wheelchair could bob for apples. Could a witch walk with a cane?

By the end of the Scout meeting, most of the Pee Wees were smiling again. They said the Pee Wee Scout pledge. It made Molly remember what being a Pee Wee Scout was all about. Then they sang the Pee Wee Scout song.

"We will meet them next Tuesday," said Mrs. Peters. "At Crestwood Nursing Home."

Molly was shocked at Mrs. Peters's words. Now she was not smiling. She felt like crying.

"I'm not going to that party," she said to Mary Beth on the way home.

"Why not?" Mary Beth demanded. "It won't be so bad."

"It will be awful!" cried Molly. "My grandpa is in Crestwood Nursing Home. And he is the grumpiest person I know."

Molly began to cry. Then she began to tell Mary Beth how her grandpa had yelled at her one day at dinner. "He said, 'Take your elbows off the table. We have to remember manners in this family.' I'm scared of him," sobbed Molly.

Mary Beth tried to make Molly feel better. But she didn't know what to say. "You have to come to the party," she said.

When Molly got home, she went to her room.

She slammed the door.

Then she kicked her bed.

"This will be the worst Halloween ever," she said aloud.

She thought of her grumpy grandpa.

She thought of the grumpy Halloween ahead.

Even the pumpkins would be grumpy in a nursing home.

Grumpy was no fun. Especially grumpy grandpas. Why did the party have to be at Crestwood Nursing Home? There were plenty of other homes in town.

The next Tuesday the Pee Wees were excited about visiting the nursing home. They talked about it during school. They couldn't wait until three o'clock.

Molly could wait. She wished three o'clock would never come.

After school, some of the Pee Wee Scouts sat together on the school bus. They sat in the back. The ride was bumpy.

"My mom said Mrs. Peters had a good idea, having the party at Crestwood," said Rachel. "She said those people need children around."

A hex on Rachel's mother. It was easy for her to say Crestwood was a good place to go. She didn't have a grumpy grandpa there.

The ride to the home went fast. Soon

Peters held up her hand. "Before go in," she said, "let's remember to polite. Don't run in the halls and don't be noisy, in case some of the people are sleeping."

Sleeping! At three o'clock in the afternoon? Molly felt queasy.

"They'll probably fall asleep during the party," said Tracy.

Some of the Scouts started snoring.

Mrs. Peters frowned. "Today we want to meet the people and cheer them up a little. Remember, it is a chance for all the Pee Wees to do a good deed. To make them less lonely."

A nurse in a white uniform met them at the door. She smiled a lot as she talked.

Smile, smile, smile.

It might be fun to be a nurse, thought Molly. She looked happy in her white uniform and big smile. The nurse told them her name was Mrs. Martin.

"Some of the people can't get out of bed," she said. "We will go to their rooms. Then we'll visit the others in the recreation room."

"I don't like how it smells in here," said Rachel, wrinkling up her nose.

Mrs. Peters put her finger on her lips and said, "Shhh."

The other Pee Wees were making faces too. It smelled like medicine and food and bathroom cleaner all at once.

Mrs. Peters gave them a warning glance.

The Scouts went from room to room, meeting the people who stayed in their beds.

The lady in the first room had no teeth.

"How does she eat?" whispered Tracy.

Mrs. Peters said, "Shhh" again.

The lady showed the Scouts pictures of

17

her grandchildren. "My grandson is in second grade too," she said proudly.

The man in the next room had his TV on. "I'll turn it off," he said. "I'd rather have company."

He asked the Scouts their names and then he told them a story of when he used to work on the railroad. Roger told him about their mascot, Lucky. And Patty told about winning the Pee Wee Scout football game.

The lady in the next room said she used to be a dancer.

"Wow!" said Rachel. "I'd like to be a ballerina."

The lady told her what steps to practice. And what shows to go to see.

"She doesn't seem old," said Rachel to Molly. "When you hear her talk."

Mrs. Peters smiled.

Then they all went to the recreation

room. There were people in wheelchairs. With walkers. And some on crutches.

"I had crutches once," said Molly. She told a man named Chuck about her sprained ankle.

The nurse brought cookies and milk. Soon Molly didn't feel scared anymore. Or mad. But where was her grandpa?

She ran up to the nurse. "Do you know Amos Duff?" she asked. "He is my grandpa. He lives here."

"Yes," said Mrs. Martin, smiling. "Amos is in the therapy room. He is having treatments on his leg. He goes every afternoon at this time."

It looked as if Molly would not see her grandpa today. After all her worrying. But she would have to see him at the party.

CHAPTER 3

A Devil and a Diver

"It's time to leave," said Mrs. Peters. "Soon it will be dinnertime for everyone here."

Molly was surprised that she wanted to stay longer. She didn't want to leave. Some of the people were fun. Some of them told good stories.

"Can't we stay a little longer?" pleaded Sonny.

"I want to hear the rest of this war story," said Roger, who was sitting next to a soldier.

"We'll be back for the party," said Mrs. Peters.

As they left, Rachel said, "They're just like real people."

"They are real people, dummy," said Roger.

"I mean like regular people," said Rachel. "Even if they do sleep a lot."

"Where was your grandpa?" asked Mary Beth.

"He was getting treatments on his leg," said Molly. "I won't see him till the party."

The ride home went fast.

The whole week went fast.

At the next meeting of the Pee Wee Scouts, they planned the party.

A party meant decorations.

Balloons. Pumpkins. Skeletons.

Goblins. Candles.

Moans and groans.

And food. The moms would send food.

Most of all, a party meant costumes. The nurses would help the seniors make their costumes, Mrs. Peters told them. But the Pee Wees had to make their own.

"I want to be sure no one knows who I am," said Tracy.

"Remember," Mrs. Peters said, "you do not have to spend a lot of money on costumes. You can make them from some old clothes or other things you have around the house. Just buy your masks at the store."

"Let's make our costumes together," said Lisa to Molly.

"Okay, and maybe we could make a costume for Tim," added Molly. "Otherwise he has to come as a Scout."

Lisa frowned. "Making three is a lot of work."

"Pooh," said Molly. "It will be easy."

That evening after dinner, Molly called

Tim on the telephone. "I'm making my costume for the party," she said. "I can make you one too."

"Then you'll know who I am," said Tim.

"I won't tell," she said. "Anyway, I'd know who you were if you came as a Scout. Everyone would."

"Okay," said Tim. "But I want to be a deep-sea diver like this guy I saw on TV." Tim paused. "They wear these big rubber feet and a big suit and this thing coming out of their head for air."

"It would be easier to make a ghost costume or something," Molly said.

"I don't want to be a ghost!" cried Tim. "I don't want to go if I'm a ghost."

"All right," said Molly.

If it wasn't for me, Tim wouldn't have a costume at all, thought Molly. Rat's knees, he should be glad to be a ghost!

*　　*　　*

The next day, Lisa came over to Molly's after school. She brought some old clothes from her grandma's trunk.

"I won't even have to make one," she said. "I'll just dress like someone from the olden days."

Molly got out the old clothes her mother said she could use. She got out some leftover material too. Molly's mother liked to sew.

The girls tried on dress after dress.

Some were too long.

Some were too big.

They all looked funny.

Finally Lisa picked a dress. It was a *Little House on the Prairie* dress.

"You need a mask to cover your face," said Molly.

"I'll buy one," Lisa said.

"Should I be a witch?" asked Molly.

Lisa shook her head. "Witches are boring."

The girls looked through the rest of the clothes and scraps.

"How about an angel?" said Lisa, pointing to a white dress.

"Naw," said Molly. "I don't like angels."

"A devil!" shouted Lisa. "This witch dress could be a devil suit if we made some legs and arms."

A devil sounded good to Molly. She would like to have horns. And carry a pitchfork.

Molly and Lisa worked all day cutting and sewing.

Snip, snip, snip.

Fold, fold, fold.

"You need long arms on it and a long red tail," said Lisa.

"And I'll need a red cap with horns on it," said Molly.

The girls made horns out of cardboard. When they were all through, Molly tried on the costume. One sleeve hung down to the ground. The other one only reached to her elbow. The horns hung down over her face!

"Rat's knees!" said Molly. "It's hard to make a costume."

"If we were rich, we could buy one," said Lisa.

"My mom wouldn't let me spend money for a whole costume," said Molly.

"Mine either," said Lisa.

Molly took off the devil suit and cut off the long sleeve. She sewed it onto the short sleeve. Then she pinned the horns back so they would stand up. Finally the costume fit.

"I don't look like a devil," sobbed Molly. "I look like a red mouse with a long tail."

"You could go as a mouse," said Lisa helpfully.

"I want to be a devil!" cried Molly, stamping her foot.

"If you get a pitchfork, you will look like a devil," said Lisa.

The girls ran out into the garage. There

was a pitchfork! Molly's dad used it in the garden.

"You're really scary now!" said Lisa.

"Good," said Molly.

The girls cleaned up their mess. Then it was time for Lisa to go home.

"I have to make Tim's costume tomorrow," said Molly, wishing she had not thought of it. Lisa was right. Costumes were a lot of work.

When Molly's dad came home from work, he said, "That pitchfork is too dangerous. You can't take that to a party."

Molly moped. Her costume was no good without a pitchfork.

After supper, Molly's dad went down into the basement. When he came up later, he had a pitchfork for Molly.

It wasn't a real one. Mr. Duff made it out of an old shovel. But it worked! It looked just like a pitchfork. And it wasn't dangerous.

Molly hugged her dad. She could never have made a pitchfork. She was having enough trouble making costumes.

The next morning at school Tim came running up to Molly. "Have you got it?" he demanded. "Where's my diver's suit?"

"Rat's knees!" said Molly. "I haven't made it yet. I had to make my own first."

Tim looked mad. He kicked a soda can on the playground.

31

"I'll make it this afternoon," said Molly.
Everyone on the playground was talking about costumes. But nobody gave away secrets.

"Mine is really fancy," said Rachel. "I'm going to win the prize for the best one."

At three o'clock, Molly groaned. She had to go home and make Tim's diver's suit. She didn't know how to do it. She needed some help.

On the way home, she told Patty about her promise to Tim.

"I know," said Patty. "Kenny's got this old snowmobile suit he outgrew. Tim is smaller than Kenny. It will make a good diver's suit. It will just need some feet and a thing on the head."

Molly felt relieved.

Patty ran home for the suit. When she came to Molly's house, she offered to help.

The suit was silvery gray. Just right. And it had a hood that could be part of the helmet. All Tim needed to buy was a face mask.

The girls thought and thought about what to use for feet, and for goggles and the air hose.

"We could make feet out of paper," said Molly.

Patty shook her head. "They would tear," she said sensibly. "They have to be made out of something strong."

The girls thought hard. "How about old boots?" said Patty. "Old big boots of your dad's?"

"Great idea!" said Molly.

The girls rushed down to the basement. They found some old hunting boots. They were big. Big enough for diver's feet.

"I'll ask him tonight," said Molly. "I'm sure it's okay to use them."

"Now the hard part," said Patty. "The air hose. Tim has to breathe underwater."

Molly looked at her mother's old vacuum cleaner standing in a corner. When she got her new one, Mrs. Duff put the old one downstairs. "How about this?" said Molly, grabbing the hose.

"Just right," said Patty. "It can be the diver's air hose."

"How will it stay on?" asked Molly.

"Tim can tie it on," said Patty. "With a rope or something."

Now Molly was excited. Tim's costume was ready. She had saved him from coming to the party as a Scout. It would have been the same as coming as himself. With no costume.

That evening, Molly asked her parents about the boots and the hose. Her dad said, "Fine. Those old boots have a leak in them. I can't wear them anymore."

And her mom said, "That is a good idea about the vacuum-cleaner hose. It's a good air tube."

The next day, Molly took the diver's suit to school in a bag. She explained how it worked.

"You have to tie the hose on," she said.

Tim frowned. "What if it falls off when I'm underwater?" he said. "I could drown."

Molly stamped her foot. "Don't be dumb, Tim. You aren't going in real water with it."

"I want a real one," he said. "Someday I might be a real diver."

"Then you'll have to get another suit," said Molly. "Those boots leak."

"I can't have leaky feet!" he cried. He looked very upset.

"Rat's knees!" said Molly. "You are lucky to have any feet at all." She turned and walked away. She would never do another good deed for a Pee Wee Scout!

As she left, she heard Tim say something.

"What?" Molly said, spinning around. "What did you say?"

"I said thanks," muttered Tim with his head under the hose.

"You're welcome," said Molly. She felt a little better.

CHAPTER 4

The Perfect Pumpkin

The next Pee Wee Scout meeting was on a sunny Saturday. When the Pee Wees got to Mrs. Peters's house a bus was waiting. The bus ride went fast.

"Pumpkin time!" called Mrs. Peters when the bus stopped. The Pee Wees tumbled out.

"Mr. Riley has let us pick whatever pumpkins we wish," she said. "We must be careful in the field and not step on any. And only one pumpkin per Scout."

The Pee Wees looked around. They were standing in a big, big pumpkin field.

Mr. Riley was waiting. He had a smile on his face. He looks like a jolly pumpkin himself, Molly thought.

"You have a good time," he said. "Choose the biggest, best pumpkin you can find."

Mrs. Peters said thank you, and the Scouts thanked him too.

"I thought they'd be on trees," said Rachel. "Like apples."

"Ha!" Roger laughed. "Pumpkin trees! You're as funny as Sonny."

"I am not!" Rachel yelled, picking up a pumpkin.

"Hey, don't throw that!" Roger ducked.

Mrs. Peters said, "No pumpkin fights."

Rachel put the pumpkin down.

The Scouts scattered in the field, lifting up vines and leaves to look for pumpkins.

"Some of the best ones are hiding," called Mrs. Peters. "They are underneath."

"Where are the price tags?" shouted Tim. "These pumpkins don't have price tags."

"Pumpkins don't grow with price tags on them!" called Sonny. Now it was Sonny's turn to laugh.

"Well, you thought pumpkins came in cans," said Tim.

It was warm and sunny in the pumpkin field. Molly sat down on an extra-large pumpkin and thought about what her pumpkin should look like.

It should be big, but not too big.

It should be round. Not long and narrow. Not tipping over onto one side. It shouldn't have any marks or bruises on it.

The one she was sitting on was just right, but it was too big. Far too big. Molly couldn't even budge it.

Patty and Kenny walked by. They

already had their pumpkins. They looked exactly alike. Twin pumpkins for twin Scouts.

Molly walked up and down the rows of pumpkins. Every time she thought she saw the right one, something was the matter. It was never perfect.

"Look at mine!" shouted Tracy to Molly.

In her hand, Tracy had the smallest pumpkin Molly had ever seen.

A wee pumpkin.

A baby pumpkin.

Molly laughed. "If you had a pumpkin family, that would be the baby," she said.

"It's perfect," said Tracy.

Tracy's eyes were wet because she was allergic to something in the pumpkin field. Her nose was running too.

But she had found a perfect pumpkin.

Orange and round.

Not lopsided.

41

No marks or bruises.

But it was too small.

"Look at this!" shouted Roger.

Molly looked.

Roger was rolling a pumpkin along the path. It was the biggest pumpkin Molly had ever seen. Even bigger than the one she had been sitting on.

"I've got the biggest one here!" shouted Roger happily.

"You'll never get it on the bus," said Molly. "I'll bet you can't even lift it."

"I can too," said Roger, but he didn't try to pick it up. He rolled it a few feet farther on.

"It's too big," said Molly.

Roger didn't seem to worry. He kept pushing.

Suddenly Molly shouted, "Here is my pumpkin!"

There under a great big pumpkin leaf was the perfect pumpkin waiting for Molly.

Round.

Orange.

Medium-sized.

No bruises.

Molly broke the stem off in just the right place so that the top would have a handle. She cradled it in her arms and walked back to the bus.

All the Scouts were admiring their pumpkins.

Sonny's pumpkin was bent. It did not stand up. It was a funny shape, with lots of lumps. It had a big bruise on one side. It was an ugly pumpkin!

"Ho, ho," said Lisa, pointing to it. "What a dumb pumpkin!"

"It isn't dumb," said Sonny. "It's the best one."

"Everyone likes a different kind," said Mrs. Peters.

Soon all of the Scouts had returned. Mrs. Peters counted noses. "Someone is missing," she said.

They looked across the field. Far away they saw a Scout.

"Who is that?" said Mrs. Peters, squinting in the sun.

"It's Roger," said Molly. "He has a giant pumpkin. He can't lift it."

Mrs. Peters frowned. "Maybe some boys can help him," she said.

Tim and Sonny and Kevin and Kenny put their own pumpkins down. They ran to help Roger. With all of them pushing, the pumpkin rolled along faster.

"Wow!" said Tracy. "You got the biggest one and I got the smallest!"

It took all the boys, and the bus driver, and Mr. Riley to lift the giant pumpkin onto the bus. Roger's pumpkin had to have a seat of its own!

"It's bigger than you are!" said Molly.

The Scouts thanked Mr. Riley again, and got onto the bus.

On the way back, the Pee Wee Scouts rubbed and polished their pumpkins with their sleeves to make them shine. They couldn't wait to get back to Mrs. Peters's house to carve them.

"Let's sing our Pee Wee Scout song," said Mrs. Peters. She led Troop 23 as they sang their song over and over. Then they sang some of their favorite camp songs.

Soon the bus rolled up in front of Mrs. Peters's house. They carried their pumpkins inside. Everyone but Roger. His pumpkin wouldn't budge.

"It will have to stay on the bus," said Lisa.

"It will have to ride around every day with the bus driver!" shouted Sonny.

"That's what you get for choosing the biggest pumpkin," said Molly.

Just then, Mr. Peters came out of the house. "I'll help," he said when he saw the problem. Finally they got Roger's pumpkin into Mrs. Peters's house.

CHAPTER 5

Frowns All Around

Mrs. Peters put newspaper down on the table. She had paper towels and brown bags. She had a pumpkin carver at each place. She held one up.

"This tool is not dangerous," she said. "It will cut pumpkins but not fingers. First we will draw the face on the pumpkin with this marker." She held one up.

"First we better think about what our pumpkin should look like," said Mary Beth.

"What a good idea!" said Mrs. Peters.

"Once you cut into it, you can't change your mind."

The Scouts sat and thought. Some of them frowned. They looked at the pumpkins. They decided which was the best side for the face. Then they picked up their markers and drew the faces.

"Keep it simple," said Mr. Peters. He was helping too. "Don't make them too fancy or they will be hard to cut."

That was a smart thing to say, thought Molly. She watched Tim draw thin spiky teeth. How could he carve them? They would fall out, they were so thin.

Molly decided to make hers a grumpy pumpkin.

A grumpy grandpa pumpkin.

She drew a long mouth.

She turned the corners down.

Frown, frown, frown.

Pout, pout, pout.

It looked grumpy already.

Rachel stood beside Molly. She drew a mouth on her pumpkin that was turned down too.

"Copycat!" shouted Molly. "Mrs. Peters, Rachel is copying my pumpkin!"

"No two pumpkins will look alike when you carve them," she said. "No one can really copy your pumpkin."

But Rachel was copying. Molly put her jacket over part of her pumpkin so Rachel couldn't see.

Pretty soon there were many grumpy pumpkins. Pumpkins with turned-down mouths.

No matter what Mrs. Peters said, they all looked alike to Molly.

Rachel put eyebrows on hers that looked mean.

Kenny drew hair on his pumpkin.

Lisa put sunglasses on hers.

Tracy put her Pee Wee kerchief on her pumpkin's head! It looked like a little old lady.

After they had finished drawing, the Pee Wees used their pumpkin carvers. First they made little holes along the black marker lines. When they had made enough holes, the piece of pumpkin fell out. It was hard work.

Then the Scouts hollowed out the insides of their pumpkins.

"Yuck!" said Rachel. "Slimy seeds!"

They were slimy.

And wet and slippery.

When the pumpkins were carved, Mrs. Peters lined them up on the table. She put a little candle in each one. She pulled down the shades and lit the candles.

"Ooooo," whispered the Pee Wee Scouts. "Look how pretty they look!"

"Scary," said Sonny. "They look like evil ghosts."

"I think they look funny," said Roger, laughing out loud. "Ho, ho, Tim's pumpkin needs braces on his teeth!"

"It does not," cried Tim. "His teeth are just sharp."

"But they all look angry or sad," said Mrs. Peters. "They're all different, but they're all grumpy. Well, we have lots of grumpy pumpkins for Halloween!"

Molly looked at everyone's pumpkin there.

At Tim's with the skinny teeth.

At Rachel's with the pointed eyebrows.

At Roger's huge pumpkin. At Tracy's little bitty one.

They were funny. And they were grumpy. But hers was best.

Molly's was the perfect pumpkin.

He looked just like her grandpa.

CHAPTER 6

Bingo and Badges

The Pee Wee Scouts took their pumpkins home. All except Roger. He had to go and get his wagon. He had to pull his pumpkin home.

Molly put hers in the living-room window.

"He does look a little like Grandpa," admitted Molly's mother.

Molly counted the days until the Halloween party. She was still a little bit afraid of seeing her grandpa. But just a little. Maybe he would be more cheerful at a party.

*   *   *

At last it was Halloween. All the Pee Wee Scouts gathered at Mrs. Peters's house first. Some of the parents came too. Mrs. Peters did not have her costume on yet.

The Pee Wees jumped up and down.

The costumes were ready.

The food was ready.

Kevin's mother made an orange and black cake. Lisa's mother sent orange and black candy corn. Molly's mother made cupcakes with pumpkin faces.

Roger brought carameled apples. "These are for us," he said. "Not the old folks. The caramel might pull their false teeth out."

Some of the Scouts laughed.

Molly frowned.

"We're lucky Halloween's on a Sunday," said Lisa. "We don't have to spoil it with school."

Molly agreed. This way they had two parties. One at school on Friday. And the big costume party today.

It was dark outside when the Pee Wees got into their costumes and masks. Their parents drove them to Crestwood Nursing Home. The Scouts helped carry the food inside.

Molly picked up her long tail and threw it over her arm. She felt very nervous walking into the party. She hoped her cardboard horns wouldn't fall in her face.

All at once, she thought she was in the wrong place. This didn't look like a nursing home at all!

There were orange lanterns for lights, and black candles.

There were skeletons hanging from the ceiling.

There was spooky music playing.

Most of all, there were strange creatures walking around.

Molly shivered inside her devil suit. Who were these people? Were they old people, or Pee Wees?

Suddenly a large egg that looked like Humpty-Dumpty came up to Molly. The egg reached out a hand!

"Welcome," said the egg. The voice sounded just like Mrs. Peters's! She made a perfect Humpty-Dumpty because she was going to have a baby.

Humpty-Dumpty walked on to greet a ballet dancer in a pink tutu. Probably Rachel, thought Molly.

Suddenly a pirate with a patch over one eye whispered into Molly's ear, "Your horns look great."

Molly recognized Patty's voice.

"Look at Tim," Patty added.

Molly looked.

Across the room behind a table full of food was the deep-sea diver.

"That's a great costume," said Patty to Molly.

Molly felt proud.

Then she wondered who all these strangers were around her. Which one was her grandpa?

Molly recognized Roger's friend, the soldier. He had his war uniform on. The man was talking to a large rabbit. It must be Roger!

Molly stayed by Patty, the only one she was sure she knew.

"It feels lonely," Molly said, "when you don't know anyone."

"We do know them, we just don't know who they are," said Patty. "I think that dinosaur over there is Roger."

"I think Roger is that pink rabbit," said Molly. "Let's look for my grandpa."

"How tall is he?" asked Patty.

"Medium-tall," said Molly. "About as tall as that prince over there." Molly changed her mind. "Or maybe as tall as that clown."

Molly looked all around. "I'll never find him!" she cried. "And I don't see anyone with a grumpy face. Or a grumpy mask."

Humpty-Dumpty was calling, "Everyone line up to bob for apples."

Molly and Patty got in line. The rabbit and soldier got behind them.

"I know it's you, Roger," said Molly.

But the rabbit said, "I'm not Roger, I'm Bugs Bunny."

"He changed his voice," said Patty. "But I'll bet it is him."

Molly wasn't sure now. She wasn't sure who anyone was.

59

When they bobbed for apples, the rabbit got his ears wet.

When Tim's turn came, his vacuum-cleaner hose fell into the tub. Oops!

"Look at the clown over there with the baggy pants," said Patty.

Molly looked.

He had yarn for hair and suspenders made out of rope.

His face was painted on.

Red eyebrows.

Red circles on his cheeks.

A round fake nose.

And his blue lips were painted into a big grin.

"He sure looks jolly," said Molly. "I wonder who he is."

All of a sudden the clown came toward the girls. He came closer and closer.

"Do you know him?" asked Molly.

Patty shook her head.

Suddenly the clown reached up and pulled off his yarn hair. He took off his fake nose.

"Grandpa!" shouted Molly. She threw her arms around him and gave him a great big hug.

"You didn't know me in this costume, did you?" he said.

"I didn't know you because you didn't look—"

Molly didn't want to say "grumpy."

"You mean I don't look grumpy," said her grandpa.

Molly was surprised that her grandpa knew he was grumpy. "You look happier," said Molly.

"I'm sorry I was so grumpy," he said. "When you don't feel good you yell at people you love. I'm better now that I've had treatments for my leg. I'll be able to go home next week!"

Molly wished she had come to see her grandpa sooner. To cheer him up. She remembered how grumpy she felt when she was sick. It helped to have company.

"Let's go have some of this good punch," said her grandpa.

Molly introduced her grandpa to the other Pee Wees.

"I thought you said your grandpa was mean," said Mary Beth. "You said he yelled at you."

"When he was sick," said Molly. "But now he feels better."

"Now!" Mrs. Peters called. "We will have the prize for the best costume."

Rachel was way up in front where the judges would see her, Molly noticed.

"First," said Mrs. Peters, "we'll have the best costume from Crestwood."

She called the name of Edith Larson. Everyone clapped. A Gypsy with lots of bracelets walked up to Mrs. Peters to get her prize. It was a good costume, thought Molly.

Then everyone grew quiet.

The Pee Wees held their breath.

Molly straightened her horns.

She sat up tall.

"The prize for the best Pee Wee costume," called Mrs. Peters, "goes to Tim Noon! For his spaceman costume!"

Tim ran to the front of the room when he heard his name. He didn't hear the word "spaceman."

Mrs. Peters said, "This is a very original costume. He looks like a real Martian with antennae on top of his head and space boots. Let's all give Tim a big hand!"

Everyone clapped.

But Tim shouted, "I'm a diver! This is a diver's suit! This is my air hose!"

Everybody kept clapping.

Mrs. Peters handed Tim a package. It was a paint set. Tim took the prize, but he frowned. "This is my air hose," he said again. But no one listened to him.

"Now!" said Mrs. Peters. "We will eat!"

As the Pee Wees filled their plates with party food, Tim whispered to Molly, "I told you I don't look like a diver with these boots!"

"You do too," said Molly. She was mad. She had made the costume. She was the creative one. And Patty had helped. But Tim got the prize.

Mrs. Peters came up beside Tim with her plate. "Did you make the costume yourself?" she asked Tim.

Molly glared at Tim.

"Molly made it," he said. "And it's not a space suit. I'm a diver."

"Why, Molly, how kind of you! What a

good job you did! Yes, I can see now it's a diver's suit."

Molly felt better. "Patty helped too," she said.

After everyone had eaten, the Pee Wees played bingo with the people in the home.

"B-12," called the nurse.

Molly put a piece of candy corn on number 12.

"O-63," the nurse called. Molly had that number too. She put another piece of candy on her card. She just needed one more.

Then the nurse said, "N-21."

"BINGO!" called Molly. She had won! Won a game of bingo! Her grandpa clapped. So did all the Pee Wees. The pink rabbit whistled through its teeth. It had to be Roger!

Molly ran up to get her prize. It was a

little pocket radio. She had always wanted a radio just like it!

Rat's knees, what a fun party! Molly was glad the party was at Crestwood after all.

After the bingo game, Mrs. Peters stood up. "I have some badges to give out tonight," she said. "To some hardworking Pee Wee Scouts."

Mrs. Peters gave out a badge for carving the best pumpkin. And badges for helping to cheer up the people in the home.

Then she called Tim's name. "For the best costume," she said, handing Tim a badge. He pinned it on his shirt.

"And I also have a badge for *making* the best costume," she said. "For Molly Duff!"

Molly ran up to get her badge. What a surprise, she thought. She pinned it on her costume.

Then some of the Crestwood people began to yawn.

The Pee Wees yawned too. It was getting late.

Mrs. Peters got everyone into a big circle. It was a very big circle!

The Pee Wee Scouts held hands with the grown-ups. They all said the Pee Wee Scout pledge. Then they sang the Pee Wee Scout song.

It was time to go home.

A bingo prize, a smiling grandpa, and now a badge. For Molly, it was the best Halloween party she could remember!

♪ ♪ ♪ Pee Wee Scout Song ♪ ♪ ♪

(to the tune of
"Old MacDonald Had a Farm")

Scouts are helpers, Scouts have fun,
Pee Wee, Pee Wee Scouts!
We sing and play when work is done,
Pee Wee, Pee Wee Scouts!

With a good deed here,
And an errand there,
Here a hand, there a hand,
Everywhere a good hand.

Scouts are helpers, Scouts have fun,
Pee Wee, Pee Wee Scouts!

70

⭐ Pee Wee Scout Pledge ⭐

We love our country
And our home,
Our school and neighbors too.

As Pee Wee Scouts
We pledge our best
In everything we do.